The Elves and the Emperor

For James and Cormac

First published in 2008
by Wayland

Text copyright © Hilary Robinson 2008
Illustration copyright © Simona Sanfilippo 2008

Wayland
338 Euston Road
London NW1 3BH

Wayland Australia
Level 17/207 Kent Street
Sydney, NSW 2000

Series Editor: Louise John
Editor: Katie Powell
Cover design: Paul Cherrill
Design: D.R.ink
Consultant: Shirley Bickler

A CIP catalogue record for this book is available from the British Library.

ISBN 9780750255226

Printed in China

Wayland is a division of Hachette Children's Books,
an Hachette Livre UK Company

www.hachettelivre.co.uk

The Elves and the Emperor

Written by Hilary Robinson
Illustrated by Simona Sanfilippo

WAYLAND

There was a commotion at the palace.
"Worn-out shoes!" the emperor sighed.

"Summon the old shoemaker!
I need new shoes!" he cried.

"I've heard you have little elves
who make shoes by candlelight.

6

"Please ask them as a favour
if they'll work for me tonight.

"I have pyjamas made from silk,
and a nightcap with a feather.

"So all I need are slippers
cut from the softest leather.

9

"In return my wife, the queen,
will make the elves new suits.

"They can wear them to a party with a matching pair of boots!"

So the shoemaker cut the leather and left it out that night.

Then his elves began to stitch
and finished by first light.

They climbed out of the window and danced and skipped away.

They didn't want to be seen
when the emperor woke that day.

15

The emperor got up in the morning and went straight to his shelves.

"What perfect slippers!" he exclaimed. "Such clever little elves."

17

The emperor was delighted.
He was the smartest man in town.

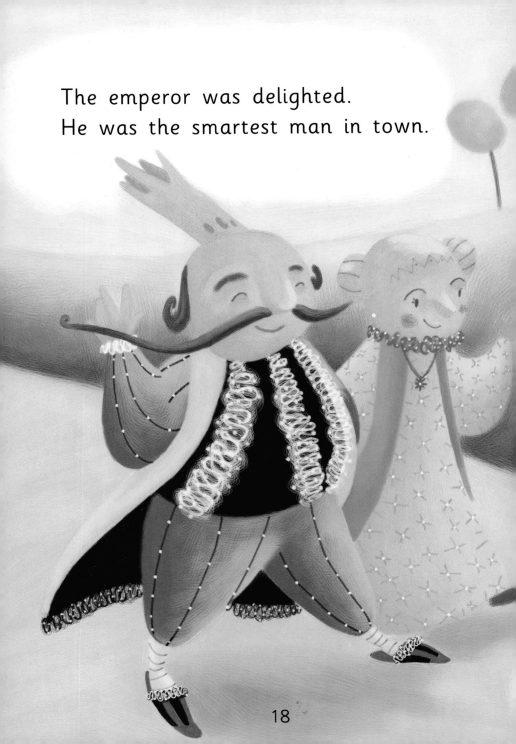

He wore his elegant slippers
with his velvet robe and crown.

He wore them to the races...

on his horse...

and on his ship.

He wore them to the market
when he made a royal trip.

He strode around the market stalls and looked at some bananas.

Suddenly a boy yelled out,
"The emperor's in pyjamas!"

He looked down at his clothes and said, "I do look rather silly. A man who is as grand as me should wear something far less frilly."

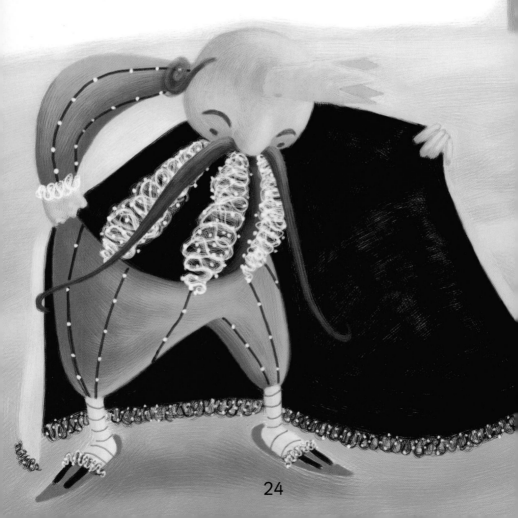

"What about a suit?" he said.
"I've got one that will fit!"

And, turning to the elves, he cried,
"I'll need shoes to go with it!"

That night the kings and queens arrived, for a feast of meat and fruit.
And the emperor made an entrance in...

...his royal swimming suit!

31

START READING is a series of highly enjoyable books for beginner readers. **The books have been carefully graded to match the Book Bands widely used in schools.** This enables readers to be sure they choose books that match their own reading ability.

Look out for the Band colour on the book in our Start Reading logo.

The Bands are:

Pink Band 1

Red Band 2

Yellow Band 3

Blue Band 4

Green Band 5

Orange Band 6

Turquoise Band 7

Purple Band 8

Gold Band 9

START READING books can be read independently or shared with an adult. They promote the enjoyment of reading through satisfying stories supported by fun illustrations.

Hilary Robinson loves jumbling up stories and seeing how they turn out. Her life is a jumbled up lot of fun, too! Hilary writes books for children and produces radio programmes for BBC Radio 2 and, because she loves doing both, she really does feel as if she is living happily ever after!

Simona Sanfilippo loves to draw and paint all kinds of animals and people. She enjoyed reading illustrated fairytales as a child, and hopes you will enjoy reading these fairytale jumbles, too!